DUDLEY SCHOOLS
LIBRARY SERVICE

KU-395-624

The Gentle Lion and the Little Owlet

Schools Library and Information Services

S00000742942

This book is dedicated to my wonderful family.

DUDLEY PUBLIC LIBRARIES

L

742942   SCH

JYSHI

This edition first published in the United Kingdom in 2012 by
Pavilion Children's Books
an imprint of Anova Books Group Ltd
10 Southcombe Street
London W14 0RA

Layout © Pavilion Children's Books
Text and illustrations © Alice Shirley

All rights reserved. No part of this publication may be reproduced,
stored in a retrieval system, or transmitted in any form or by any means
electronic, mechanical, photocopying, recording or otherwise, without the
prior written permission of the copyright owner.

A CIP catalogue record for this book is available from the British Library.

10 9 8 7 6 5 4 3 2 1

ISBN 978-1-84365-1-994

Repro by Dot Gradations Ltd, UK
Printed by Toppan Leefung Printing Ltd, China

This book can be ordered direct from the publisher at the website
www.anovabooks.com

The Gentle Lion and the Little Owlet

A TALE OF AN UNLIKELY FRIENDSHIP

Alice Shirley

PAVILION
CHILDREN'S

High up, in the tallest
tree in the zoo, two tawny
owls perched. Their nest
lay beside them, holding
four pale, delicate eggs.

Tap Scratch **Crack!**

As the sun rose, a soft sound broke the quiet.

A round amber eye peeked out at the wide world.
Soon, the other three eggs hatched and four fluffy
grey heads were whistling,

"Food! Food! Food!"

For several nights and days the parent owls
flew to and fro with food for their chicks until,
finally exhausted, they fell asleep cuddled
together in a tawny owl heap.

"I am big now," cheeped one little owlet, "I am strong. I want to see the wide world on my own!"

He

hopped

hop

hop

to the edge of the nest and spread his wings, but ...

Down

Down

Down

he fell like a fluffy round stone into the grass.

Thlump!

On either side of him was a HUGE furry paw with shiny black claws. He looked up and saw the great lion's jaws with gleaming white teeth.

"I'm sorry," he peeped, not really sorry at all. "I didn't mean to fall. I was trying to fly, but it seems I am not ready yet."

The lion was puzzled.
This fluffy thing is not
afraid of me, he thought.
Not like everyone else.

"One day, I will fly high and fly far. I want to see further than the view from our tree," cheeped the owlet, "I want to see the whole world!"

"When I was a young cub," growled the lion, "I lived in a far away land called Africa, with mountains and jungles and great grassy plains. I would love to go there again."

"When I can fly, we will!" said the owlet with a hoot.

As night painted the sky inky dark, the lion and the little owlet gazed up at the stars.

The lion told his new friend about the land in his country – the different shapes in the stars and the huge, hot African sun. The owlet listened until his fluffy head dropped. He fell asleep curled between the lion's paws.

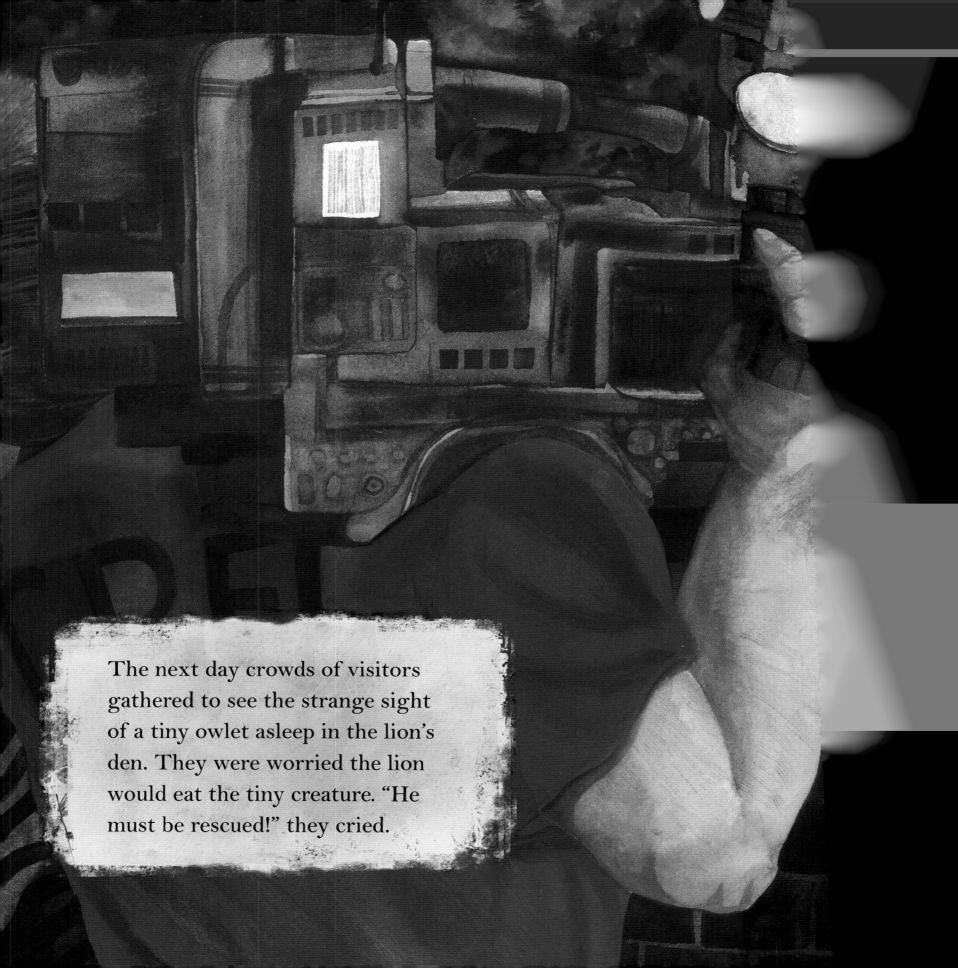

The next day crowds of visitors gathered to see the strange sight of a tiny owlet asleep in the lion's den. They were worried the lion would eat the tiny creature. "He must be rescued!" they cried.

Thump!

The owlet and the lion woke – something had landed near their heads. The zookeeper was holding a basket, full of birdseed, on a rope.

But the little owlet ignored the basket. "I don't need rescuing. I want to see the world with you," he said to the lion.

The next day the zookeeper had another rescue idea. He dressed up in an owl costume and stood on the edge of the lion enclosure, flapping and hooting. The crowd laughed.

"I *think* he wants you to fly," said the amused lion. "My wings are growing stronger," peeped the owlet, "but not enough yet. Besides, you must come with me!"

Several nights later the zookeeper tiptoed
to the gate of the lion enclosure to try and
rescue the owlet while the lion slept. But,
the lion and the owlet were not asleep.
The gate creaked as he opened it …

"NOW!" cried the owlet, and the lion leapt
past the bewildered zookeeper.

In the morning, a huge crowd flocked to
the lion's cage with their cameras
at the ready.

click, click, click

All they could see was the zookeeper sat
trembling in a corner – but neither the lion
nor the owlet could be seen anywhere.

The real story

Based on events that happened at Paignton Zoo Environmental Park, Devon, England, in June 2010.

Sheila Hassanein, a frequent visitor to the zoo, was lucky enough to be in the right place at the right time, capturing this amazing moment on camera. It began when a small tawny owl chick landed in the lion enclosure at Paignton Zoo and came face-to-face with Indu, a seven-year-old female Asiatic lion. As the crowds gathered, worries over the owlet's safety grew, but a rescue attempt was impossible because zoo keepers could not enter the enclosure.

Lions are renowned as cunning hunters. They can weigh in at up to 180 kilos while the owlet would have been a matter of grams. The owlet could have been swallowed in one easy mouthful. Indu looked at the owlet and the owlet looked at Indu – but nothing more happened.

It is thought that the owlet flew away in the night. No-one can be absolutely sure that the lion did not eat it – however, the keepers are confident that if she had, there would have been evidence in the form of fluff and feathers.

The lion and the owlet became famous, with their pictures making many national newspapers.

Paignton Zoo is a registered charity, www.paigntonzoo.org.uk.

Image © Sheila Hassanein